A Note to Parents and Caregivers:

Read-it! Readers are for children who are just starting on the amazing road to reading. These beautiful books support both the acquisition of reading skills and the love of books.

 The PURPLE LEVEL presents basic topics and objects using high frequency words and simple language patterns.

 The RED LEVEL presents familiar topics using common words and repeating sentence patterns.

 The BLUE LEVEL presents new ideas using a larger vocabulary and varied sentence structure.

 The YELLOW LEVEL presents more challenging ideas, a broad vocabulary, and wide variety in sentence structure.

 The GREEN LEVEL presents more complex ideas, an extended vocabulary range, and expanded language structures.

 The ORANGE LEVEL presents a wide range of ideas and concepts using challenging vocabulary and complex language structures.

When sharing a book with your child, read in short stretches, pausing often to talk about the pictures. Have your child turn the pages and point to the pictures and familiar words. And be sure to reread favorite stories or parts of stories.

There is no right or wrong way to share books with children. Find time to read with your child, and pass on the legacy of literacy.

Adria F. Klein, Ph.D.
Professor Emeritus
California State University
San Bernardino, California

To the parents of Michelle, Patrick, and Katherine, who are completely crazy about their kids

First American edition published in 2005 by
Picture Window Books
5115 Excelsior Boulevard
Suite 232
Minneapolis, MN 55416
877-845-8392
www.picturewindowbooks.com

First published in Canada in 2001 by
Les éditions Héritage inc.
300 Arran Street, Saint Lambert
Quebec, Canada J4R 1K5

Printed in the United States of America.

Library of Congress Cataloging-in-Publication Data
Tondreau-Levert, Louise, 1949-
Parents do the weirdest things! / Louise Tondreau-Levert ; illustrated by Rogé.
p. cm. — (Read-it! readers)
Summary: Reveals some of the strange things a mother and father do when their two
children are not at home.
ISBN 1-4048-1031-5 (hardcover)
[1. Parents—Fiction.] I. Rogé, 1972- ill. II. Title. III. Series.

PZ7.T616Par 2004
[E]—dc22   2004023778

Parents Do the Weirdest Things!

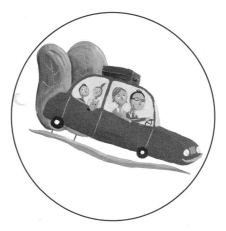

By Louise Tondreau-Levert
Illustrated by Rogé

Special thanks to our advisers for their expertise:

Adria F. Klein, Ph.D.
Professor Emeritus, California State University
San Bernardino, California

Susan Kesselring, M.A.
Literacy Educator
Rosemount - Apple Valley - Eagan (Minnesota) School District

PICTURE WINDOW BOOKS
Minneapolis, Minnesota

Mimi and I have pretty ordinary parents.

They're like the parents you see every day, just about everywhere: at the grocery store, on the bus, on the sidewalk, and even at the museum. All you have to do is take a look around.

Sometimes our parents have fun, but never until they've finished doing all sorts of boring, complicated chores.

So what do parents do when their kids aren't around?

When Grandma comes to pick us up, we always stop in the doorway. What will Mom and Dad do without us?

The last time we left them all alone, at first
they just sat there doing nothing at all.

10

But after we left, they turned the whole house upside down. They painted our bedroom walls, changed the furniture around, and put all our toys away in strange places. They even forgot to feed the dog.

Parents really do the weirdest things when their kids aren't around!

Sometimes we have other things to do, and so we leave Mom and Dad in the care of their best friends.

When that happens, they never, EVER, eat spaghetti sandwiches or sweet-onion ice cream.

13

Once they made a special dinner, just for their friends. They ate for a long, long time.

And they ate only the best food, like stinky cheese, raw fish, giant mushrooms, slimy oysters, and all sorts of creatures that live inside shells.

The next day, when Mimi and I came home, we set them free. Not Mom and Dad! The snails!

Parents really do the weirdest things when their kids aren't around!

Later on, we unwrapped the candy that
Grandma had given us. Mom and Dad
are always telling us that sweets are bad
for our teeth.

But as soon as we turned our backs,
they gobbled them up.

Parents really do the weirdest things
when their kids aren't around!

Going away to summer camp is even worse. Last summer, our parents worried about us so much that they came to spy on us. They followed us everywhere, even on the treasure hunt.

21

Unfortunately, the treasure-keeper
was a sweet little skunk.

22

Suddenly, Mom and Dad smelled pretty awful!
They went home in a big hurry.

For our birthday, we went to sleep over at
Aunt Jeanne's house. Dad promised us a
big surprise.

The next day, we discovered an awesome swimming pool ... in our bedroom! It was supposed to be in the backyard, but Dad made a few mistakes.

Parents really do the weirdest things when their kids aren't around!

While we waited for the pool movers to
come, we had to go scuba diving so we
could finish our homework. That's how
we found out that Dad's computer doesn't
work so well underwater.

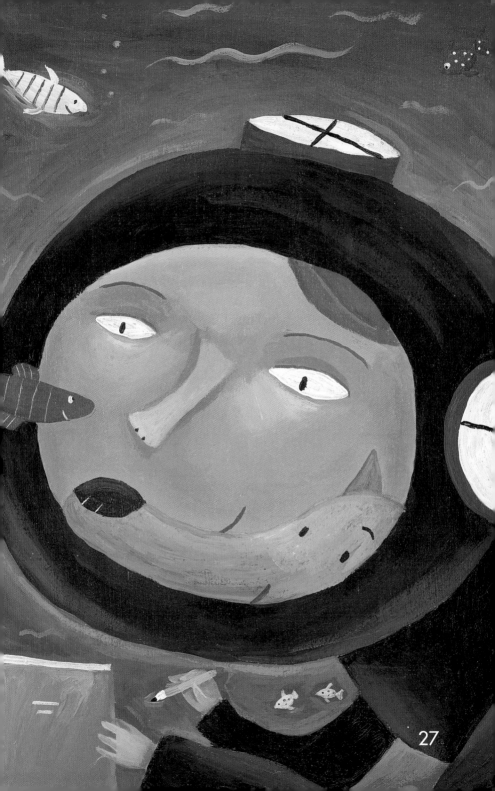

Sometimes, when we play outside, our parents just sit quietly in the house. That's when we know they're planning something really bizarre, like moving somewhere on the back of an elephant, going on a desert safari, flying in a hot-air balloon, or worse yet, having a little brother.

Parents really do the weirdest things when their kids aren't around!

29

Ever since the twins arrived, our parents are always saying that they're tired. So they take little vacations far away, really far away, in the mountains.

Then the twins, Mimi, and I have a great time!

Now, do you ever wonder what kids do when their parents aren't around?

More *Read-it!* Readers

Bright pictures and fun stories help you practice your reading skills. Look for more books at your level.

Alex and the Team Jersey by Gilles Tibo
Alex and Toolie by Gilles Tibo
Clever Cat by Karen Wallace
Daddy's a Busy Beaver by Bruno St-Aubin
Daddy's a Dinosaur by Bruno St-Aubin
Felicio's Incredible Invention by Mireille Villeneuve
Flora McQuack by Penny Dolan
Izzie's Idea by Jillian Powell
Mysteries for Felicio by Mireille Villeneuve
Naughty Nancy by Anne Cassidy
Parents Do the Weirdest Things! by Louise Tondreau-Levert
Peppy, Patch, and the Postman by Marisol Sarrazin
Peppy, Patch, and the Socks by Marisol Sarrazin
The Princess and the Frog by Margaret Nash
The Roly-Poly Rice Ball by Penny Dolan
Run! by Sue Ferraby
Sausages! by Anne Adeney
Stickers, Shells, and Snow Globes by Dana Meachen Rau
Theodore the Millipede by Carole Tremblay
The Truth About Hansel and Gretel by Karina Law
Willie the Whale by Joy Oades

Looking for a specific title or level? A complete list of *Read-it!* Readers is available on our Web site: *www.picturewindowbooks.com*